Oprah Winfrey

by Jonatha A. Brown

Reading consultant: Susan Nations, M.Ed., author/literacy coach/consultant

WEEKLY WR READER®
EARLY LEARNING LIBRARY

Please visit our web site at: www.garethstevens.com
For a free color catalog describing Weekly Reader® Early Learning Library's list
of high-quality books, call 1-877-445-5824 (USA) or 1-800-387-3178 (Canada).
Weekly Reader® Early Learning Library's fax: (414) 336-0164.

Library of Congress Cataloging-in-Publication Data

Brown, Jonatha A.
    Oprah Winfrey / by Jonatha A. Brown.
       p. cm. — (People we should know)
    Includes bibliographical references and index.
    ISBN 0-8368-4312-6 (lib. bdg.)
    ISBN 0-8368-4319-3 (softcover)
    1. Winfrey, Oprah. 2. Television personalities—United States—Biography—Juvenile literature.
3. Actors—United States—Biography—Juvenile literature. I. Title. II. People we should know (Milwaukee, Wis.)
PN1992.4.W56B78 2004
791.4502'8'092—dc22
    [B]
                                                      2004044479

This edition first published in 2005 by
Weekly Reader® Early Learning Library
A Member of the WRC Media Family of Companies
330 West Olive Street, Suite 100
Milwaukee, WI 53212 USA

Based on *Oprah Winfrey* (Trailblazers of the Modern World series) by Jean F. Blashfield
Editor: JoAnn Early Macken
Designer: Scott M. Krall
Picture researcher: Diane Laska-Swanke

Photo credits: Cover, title, pp. 9, 14 Photofest; pp. 4, 5, 13, 19 © AP/Wide World Photos; p. 7 © Gini Holland;
p. 11 © Reuters; p. 15 © Touchstone Pictures/Courtesy of Getty Images; p. 17 © Cynthia Johnson/Getty
Images; p. 18 Courtesy of Getty Images; p. 21 © Jeff Christensen/Reuters

Printed in the United States of America

3 4 5 6 7 8 9 10 09 08 07 06

Table of Contents

Words that appear in the glossary are printed in **boldface**
type the first time they occur in the text.

Chapter 1: A Shaky Start

Oprah Winfrey is a rich and famous woman. But when she was young, she was poor.

Oprah Winfrey was born on January 29, 1954. She was born in Mississippi. Oprah's parents were not married. Her mother was very young. She still lived with her own parents. Oprah lived with them, too. She called her grandmother "Momma."

The family lived on a tiny farm. There they had a garden and raised a few pigs and chickens. They were very poor.

This photo shows Oprah with Phil Donahue. He is another famous talk show host. Their shows were on TV at the same time.

Oprah was smart. She could read when she was three years old. She liked to learn stories by heart and **recite** them. Oprah recited Bible stories in church. When no one else would listen, she put on shows for the pigs and chickens.

Oprah's mother moved to Wisconsin when Oprah was four years old. Oprah stayed behind with Momma. Momma was not gentle or kind. She did not hug or kiss Oprah. When Oprah was bad, Momma hit her. Those beatings really hurt.

Moving to Milwaukee

When Oprah was six, she joined her mother in Wisconsin. They lived in the city of Milwaukee. They were just as poor in the city as they had been in the country. Oprah's mother worked as a maid all day. She went out at night. She did not spend much time with her little girl.

Oprah's mother had another child. Her name was Patricia. She was Oprah's half sister. Later, Oprah had a half brother, too.

Oprah spent one year in Nashville, Tennessee. Her father and stepmother lived there. They paid attention to her. They helped her with her schoolwork. Oprah was in third grade.

This photo shows Oprah at age thirteen. It is from her school yearbook.

After that year, she moved back in with her mother. There, Oprah could do as she pleased, but she did not feel loved.

Years passed, and Oprah became a teen. In high school, she was quiet. She read a lot of books. She rode three buses to get to a good school. Then she saw how other people lived. She saw a better world outside the **ghetto**. She also saw how poor her family was.

Troubled Times

Oprah's teen years were hard. She had no one to guide her. She started to get into trouble. She stole money from her mother. She even ran away from home.

Oprah was out of control. So her mother sent Oprah back to Nashville. She moved in with her father again.

Chapter 2: Oprah Blossoms

Living with her father was a big change for Oprah. He and his wife kept a close eye on her. They told Oprah when to be home. They made her do her homework and go to church. Oprah did not like that at first. Then she began to work hard and feel proud of herself. She decided she would be the best she could be.

Oprah grew up in a ghetto. Many years later, she made and starred in a movie about two African American boys who lived in a ghetto. The movie was called *There Are No Children Here*.

Oprah read books, studied hard, and got high grades. She began to recite in church again. She was so good that people came just to hear her. People invited her to speak at other churches. She traveled to California and Colorado. She even won a local talent contest. After that, she was asked to read the news on a radio station. She worked at the station after school.

College Life

In 1971, Oprah was ready for college. But it had only been four years since she had been so wild. Her father did not trust her. He did not want her to be on her own yet. So Oprah went to college in Nashville. There she took classes in acting. She acted in many plays. She still spent a lot of time reading.

Oprah makes all kinds of people feel welcome on her show. Here she is talking with First Lady Laura Bush.

She was still in college when she got a chance to be on TV. A local station needed someone to read the news. People at the station heard about Oprah. They asked her to try out for the job.

Soon Oprah was on the air! She was the first female news reporter on TV in Nashville. She was also the first black news reporter there. She worked at the station for three years.

Another Change

After college, Oprah was on her own. She moved to Maryland to work for a TV station. At first, she was a news reporter. It was not an easy job. Soon, though, the people at the station asked her to change jobs. They asked her to **cohost** a talk show. That show was called *People Are Talking*.

Being on a talk show was more fun than reading the news. Oprah could really be herself. She liked talking to the guests. She got along well with her cohost. More people started watching the show. "This is what I really should have been doing all along," Oprah said.

Chapter 3: Making a Difference

Oprah relaxed in her Chicago office in 1985.

In 1984, Oprah moved again. This time she went to Chicago, Illinois. She hosted another TV talk show.

The show was called *A.M. Chicago*. Before Oprah came, viewers did not like that show very much. When she started hosting it, they changed their minds. Her lively, caring ways made the show a huge success. Its name was changed to *The Oprah*

Oprah includes the audience in her TV shows.

Winfrey Show. People all over the country watched it. In three years, it became the most popular talk show on TV.

TV viewers loved Oprah for many reasons. She really listened when her guests talked. She laughed when they said something funny. She cried when they talked about terrible or sad things. She made it safe for people to talk about their feelings.

Oprah and Danny Glover starred in the 1998 movie *Beloved*.

She said that everyone has problems. She said that having problems does not make people bad.

After she moved to Chicago, Oprah branched out. She acted in movies. She worked with famous people. She liked working on movies very much. Soon she formed her own movie company. She called it Harpo Productions. "Harpo" is "Oprah" spelled backwards.

Working to Help Others

By that time, Oprah was very rich. But riches and fame were not enough for her. She wanted to make the world a better place, too. Oprah remembered how adults had hurt her when she was a child. Her grandmother had hurt her. Men had hurt her. And she knew that adults were still hurting children. So she began to speak out, and she worked for change. Oprah helped us get better laws that protect children.

In 1993, President Bill Clinton signed a law to protect children. The law is called the "Oprah Bill." Oprah watched him sign it.

Oprah wanted to do still more. She decided to set up a group to help others. She called it the Oprah Winfrey Foundation. Her group gives money to good causes. It helps women, children, and families all over the world.

Chapter 4: She Never Stops

Oprah publishes *O* magazine. She appears on the cover each month.

Years have gone by. Oprah keeps reaching out to people in new ways. In 1996, she began sharing her love of books with her fans. Each month, she told viewers about a book she liked. She gave them a few weeks to read it. Then she invited the person who wrote the book to be on her show. She and her audience discussed the book with its **author**. She called these shows "Oprah's Book Club." Soon people all over the country were reading the books in Oprah's Book Club.

The next year, she started Oprah's Angel Network. This group grants money to good causes. Oprah gives part of her own pay to the network. She asks people who watch her show to give money, too.

The Angel Network helps people in need. This girl is going to a hospital to get the care she needs.

"I want you to open your hearts and see the world in a different way," Oprah has told them. "I promise this will change your life for the better."

Awards and Honors

Oprah Winfrey and her show have won thirty-nine Emmy awards. They honor excellence in television production. Here are some of the other awards Oprah has received for her wonderful work.

1988: International Radio and Television Society Broadcaster of the Year

1993: Horatio Alger Award for overcoming poverty and **adversity**

1998: Emmy for Lifetime Achievement

2002: Bob Hope **Humanitarian** Award

2003: Marian Anderson Award for helping **minority** students and families

The Angel Network has raised millions of dollars. That money helps send poor children to college. It helps build schools and houses in poor areas, too.

Oprah is not finished yet. She keeps working hard. She keeps using her skills in new ways. And she keeps helping others help themselves.

Oprah has been given many awards for her TV show. Here she is holding an Emmy award.

Glossary

adversity — bad luck

author — a person who has written a book

cohost — to be one of a pair of people who receive guests on a radio or television program, or one of the people in such a pair

ghetto — a part of a city where members of a minority group live, often because of poverty

humanitarian — a person who works for the good of other people

minority — a member of a group whose skin color or background is different from that of the larger group around it

recite — to speak words learned by heart

For More Information

Books

A is for Abigail: An Almanac of Amazing American Women. Lynne Cheney (Simon & Schuster Children's Publishing)

Oprah Winfrey: Media Superstar. Kristen Woronoff (Gale Group)

Oprah Winfrey: Success with an Open Heart. Tanya Lee Stone (Millbrook)

The Oprah Winfrey Story: Speaking Her Mind. Geraldine Woods (Dillon Press)

Web Sites

Academy of Achievement

www.achievement.org/autodoc/page/win0int-1
Interview with Oprah

Encarta Encyclopedia Center

encarta.msn.com/encyclopedia_761578521/Oprah_Winfrey.html
Oprah Winfrey encyclopedia article

Oprah.com: Live Your Best Life

www.oprah.com
Oprah's official web site

Index

About the Author

Jonatha A. Brown has written several books for children. She lives in Phoenix, Arizona, with her husband and two dogs. If you happen to come by when she isn't at home working on a book, she's probably out riding or visiting with one of her horses. She may be gone for quite a while, so you'd better come back later.